EARLY BIRD
STORIES™

Seeds
&
Stuck in
the Tree

Early★Reader

First American edition published in 2019 by Lerner Publishing Group, Inc.

An original concept by Jenny Jinks
Copyright © 2019 Jenny Jinks

Illustrated by Kathryn Selbert

First published by Maverick Arts Publishing Limited

Maverick
arts publishing

Licensed Edition
Seeds & Stuck in the Tree

Lerner Publications Company
A division of Lerner Publishing Group, Inc.
241 First Avenue North
Minneapolis, MN 55401 USA

For reading levels and more information, look up this title at www.lernerbooks.com.

Main body text set in Mikado a. Typeface provided by HVD Fonts.

Library of Congress Cataloging-in-Publication Data

The Cataloging-in-Publication Data for *Seeds & Stuck in the Tree* is on file at the Library of Congress.
ISBN 978-1-5415-4165-8 (lib. bdg.)
ISBN 978-1-5415-4628-8 (pbk.)
ISBN 978-1-5415-4321-8 (eb pdf)

Manufactured in the United States of America
1-45339-38989-6/22/2018

Seeds
&
Stuck in the Tree

Jenny Jinks

Illustrated by
Kathryn Selbert

Lerner Publications ◆ Minneapolis

The Letter "P"

Trace the lowercase and uppercase letter with a finger. Sound out the letter.

Down,
up,
around

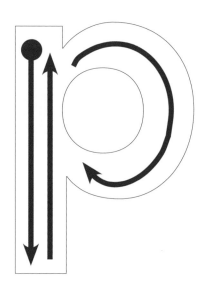

Down,
up,
around

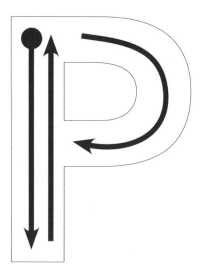

Some words to familiarize:

seeds   plant   water

High-frequency words:

is go in the a on no

Tips for Reading *Seeds*

- Practice the words listed above before reading the story.

- If the reader struggles with any of the other words, ask them to look for sounds they know in the word. Encourage them to sound out the words and help them read the words if necessary.

- After reading the story, ask the reader what Tim and Pip's seeds grew into.

Fun Activity

Plant carrot or sunflower seeds of your own.

Seeds

Tim is big.

Pip is not.

Tim and Pip get some seeds.

Tim's seed is big.

Pip's seed is not.

Tim and Pip get big pots.

The seeds go in the pot.

Tim and Pip water the seeds.

Tim tips in a lot.

Pip tips in a bit.

Tim and Pip check on the plants.

Tim's plant is big.

Pip's plant is not.

Tim and Pip love their plants.

No, this plant is the best!

The Letter "K"

Trace the lowercase and uppercase letter with a finger. Sound out the letter.

Down,
lift,
down,
down

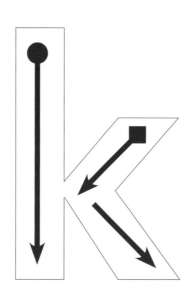

Down,
lift,
down,
down

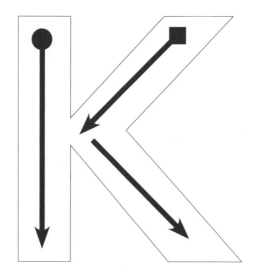

Some words to familiarize:

tree   stuck   climb

High-frequency words:

is in the said are they a up

Tips for Reading *Stuck in the Tree*

- Practice the words listed above before reading the story.
- If the reader struggles with any of the other words, ask them to look for sounds they know in the word. Encourage them to sound out the words and help them read the words if necessary.
- After reading the story, ask the reader if they remember who was stuck in the tree.

Fun Activity

Ask the reader how they would get down if they were stuck in a tree.

Stuck in the Tree

Kit is in the tree.

"Get down," says Dad.
But Kit is stuck.

Dad climbs the tree.

Now Kit and Dad
are in the tree.

"Get down," says Ben.
But they are stuck.

Ben climbs the tree.